WONDROUS PLANT & EARTH EXPERIMENTS

Q.L. PEARCE

Illustrated by
TONY GLEESON

TOR

A TOM DOHERTY ASSOCIATES BOOK
NEW YORK

SUPER SCIENCE EXPERIMENTS
published by Tor Books
Amazing Energy Experiments
Wondrous Plant and Earth Experiments

WONDROUS PLANT AND EARTH EXPERIMENTS

Copyright © 1989 by RGA Publishing Group

A TOR Book
Published by Tom Doherty Associates, Inc.
49 West 24 Street
New York, NY 10010

ISBN: 0-812-59389-8   Can. ISBN: 0-812-59390-1

First edition: September 1989

Book design by Stacey Simons/Neuwirth & Associates

Printed in the United States of America

0   9   8   7   6   5   4   3   2   1

CONTENTS

NOTE TO PARENTS

Super Science Experiments / Wondrous Plants and Earth Experiments is the perfect supplement to the classroom science curriculum. It is filled with hands on experiments that will spark your child's interest and curiosity about his or her environment. Each activity has been designed to be safe and simple, requiring materials that are inexpensive and readily available. If possible, provide an area where often-used items may be stored. Some experiments may be a little messy and those that involve heat, sharp instruments, and/or an outdoor space may require adult supervision or participation. At the beginning of the book, there is a list of equipment that is needed to perform many of the experiments, followed by a section on safety sense. It is a good idea to review these segments with your child before he or she begins the first activity. After an experiment has been completed, ask questions about how and why it worked as it did. Encouraging youngsters to formulate their own ideas will promote understanding of the basic concept illustrated by the experiment.

ABOUT THIS BOOK

Why do icebergs float? Why do plants' leaves grow upward and the roots downward? Things happen for reasons that may not be clear at first. Men and women are working in every branch of science to discover the answers. The best way to find out is through observation, and by performing an experiment. First you must have a question, then think of a way to find the answer. Each of the experiments that follow starts with a question. Read the activity through completely before you begin, and be sure that you have all of the materials at hand. Sometimes finding an answer will lead to more questions. If so, go ahead and design your own experiments and keep a notebook to record your results. HAVE FUN!

YOUR SCIENCE LAB

The kitchen is the best place to perform most experiments because running water is available. In some cases you may need to heat things on the stove, or cool them in the refrigerator. Many of your supplies are probably already in your house. Ask an adult before you use household materials.

Here is a list of some of the items you may need for your nature laboratory:

- Chopping board for cutting.
- Salt, food coloring, baking soda, vinegar, sugar, liquid detergent.
- Saucepan, pie plate, clean glass jam or jelly jars with lids, measuring cups, measuring spoons, wooden spoon, drinking glass, mixing bowls.
- String, tape, paper clips, balloons, rubber bands, scissors, knife, eyedropper, thermometer, stopwatch or clock with a second hand, tweezers, rubber tubing, compass, magnifying glass, small glass tank.
- Hot pad, gloves, apron, newspaper, notebook, pencils, marking pen, drawing compass.
- Plaster of paris, potting soil, lima beans, alum, and limewater. The last two items can be purchased at a pharmacy. It is a good idea to have several growing plants ready for use. Geraniums are an excellent sample potted plant. Elodea, a water plant available at pet stores that sell tropical fish, is also useful.

For certain experiments, you may need some materials that are not mentioned here. Read through the list at the beginning of each activity before you begin.

SAFETY SENSE

Here are a few simple rules that you should *always* follow in your laboratory.

1. Read the experiment through completely before you begin.
2. Wear old clothing or an apron.
3. Cover your work area with newspaper.
4. Never put unknown material in your mouth or near your eyes.
5. Clean your work area and instruments when you are finished.
6. Wash your hands after each experiment.
7. If an experiment lasts over a long period of time, find a place where it will not be in the way of other family members.
8. Take care not to harm living things that are involved in your experiments.
9. For some experiments you may need adult help. These are marked with this symbol: ✳

WHAT IS SCIENCE?

Science is the study of the Universe and everything in it, big or small, new or old. Scientists who study *nature* are concerned with the materials that make up Earth, the events that shape it, and the plants and animals that live on it. Our Earth is unlike any other planet in the Solar System because it is the only one known to support life. Living things inhabit the air, land, and sea. Any place on the planet where life is found, from the deepest waters of the ocean to the highest mountain top, is a part of Earth's BIOSPHERE.

The first living things to appear on Earth were probably microscopic single-celled organisms much like bacteria. These eventually developed into an algalike form now known as blue-greens. The blue-greens contained a substance called chlorophyll. With this they were able to absorb light from the Sun and convert it to energy. The energy was used to convert carbon dioxide gas and water to food. This process is called PHOTOSYNTHESIS.

Except for fungi, modern plants use photosynthesis to produce food, too. Let's start our experiments by finding out more about plants.

PLANTS

THE SEED

Is the seed useful to plants after they have sprouted?

Materials:

6 lima beans (frozen or fresh)	glass jar 2 small pots paper towels	blotting paper potting soil scissors

Procedure:

1. Soak the lima beans overnight in fresh water.
2. Line the inside of the jar with the blotting paper. Stuff the center with paper towels and fill the jar with water. After a moment, pour out the water. Slip the beans in between the blotting paper and the glass.
3. After the beans sprout (in about one week), carefully remove the young plants and plant three in one pot and three in the other. When the plants are about an inch tall, clip the seeds away from those in one of the pots. Be careful not to clip the leaves. Leave the other three plants as they are. Put both pots in a sunny spot and keep the soil moist.
4. After a week, are the plants different? Do the plants with the seeds look better? Why? Is there something in the seed that the young plant needs?

WHAT'S HAPPENING HERE? When most seed-bearing plants first sprout, they are unable to use photosynthesis to make food. These young plants get nourishment from the food stored in the seed.

MORE WAYS THAN ONE

Do plants only grow from seeds?

Materials:

2 jars   knife   white potato
carrot (with some of the green top on it)

Procedure:

1. Cut the carrot about an inch from the top. Fill one of the jars with about one-half inch of water. Place the carrot in the jar, cut side down. What part of the plant

does the carrot come from? What do you think will happen?

2. Cut the potato into sections. Be sure that each section has an "eye." Put some two or three potato pieces in a glass jar with one-half inch of water in the bottom. What part of the plant does the potato come from?

3. Put both jars in a sunny place. Add water when needed. After two or three days, what happens?

WHAT'S HAPPENING HERE? You do not always have to plant seeds to grow a new plant. Some kinds of plants can grow from a section of the parent such as the leaves, stems, or roots. Other plants, such as mushrooms and ferns, grow from special cells called spores.

PLANTS FROM SPORES

Where do spores come from?

Materials:

1 can of tomato soup	3 small bowls	bread crumbs
dried leaves	magnifying glass	plastic wrap
		dust

4 *Procedure:*

1. Put a small amount of tomato soup in each bowl. Sprinkle bread crumbs in one bowl, place some dried leaves in another, put some dust (maybe you can find some in the corner of a closet) in the third plate.

2. Cover each dish with plastic wrap and keep them in a dark closet for three to five days, then examine each. What do you see? The mold growing there are small plants that grew from spores. How did the spores get into the soup? Do you think spores are carried in the air?

3. After two or three more days, examine your mold garden under the magnifying glass. Can you see the tiny plants?

WHAT'S HAPPENING HERE? Tiny spores may float in the air and spread over great distances. They can survive for a long time under unfavorable conditions. When the spores finally come in contact with a substance that enables them to produce new plants, they do.

TAKE A DEEP BREATH

Do plants need air?

Materials:

2 small green potted plants, 2 or 3 inches tall
1 pint jar

Procedure:

1. Place both plants side by side in a window that is not in direct sunlight.
2. Put the pint jar upside-down over one plant. Be sure that the jar covers the plant only and not the whole pot. That way you can water the plant without removing the jar and letting any air in.
3. For a few days care for both plants in the same manner. Keep the soil moist but not wet. What do you think will happen to the plant in the jar?
4. After two or three days, do the plants look different? Which plant is no longer healthy? Why?
5. Remove the jar so the plant receives a supply of air after a little while. What happens to the plant that was covered? Do plants need air?

WHAT'S HAPPENING HERE? Green plants need carbon dioxide from the air. Using the energy from sunlight, plants combine carbon dioxide with water to produce the simple sugars the plant uses as food.

AIR PASSAGES

How does the air get into the plant?

Materials:

1 potted green plant with at least 5 or 6 leaves
petroleum jelly

Procedure:

1. Keep the plant in a dark closet for two days.
2. Now put the plant in a sunny spot.

Coat one of the leaves on both sides with petroleum jelly. Coat another leaf only on the underside. Put petroleum jelly only on the top of a third leaf. Will the petroleum jelly prevent air from entering the plant?

3. Check the plant after a few days. What has happened to the leaves? Which leaves have dried? Do you think the openings (called stoma) through which plants breathe are located on the top or the bottom of the leaf? Why?

WHAT'S HAPPENING HERE? There are hundreds of tiny openings called STOMATA in the leaves and sometimes in the stems of green plants. Carbon dioxide enters the plant through these openings.

WATERWAYS

Where does water enter plants?

Materials:

2 small potted
    green plants
aluminum foil
marking pen

Procedure:

1. Set both plants aside and do not water them for five days.
2. Cover the soil of one pot completely with foil from the stem of the plant to the edge. Mark this pot number

one. Tip the pot and run the stem and leaves of the plant under a gentle stream of water. Be sure not to get any water in the soil.

3. Mark the second pot number two and water the plant through the soil as usual.

4. Set both in a sunny window. After two days repeat the watering process. What has happened to the two plants? Do you think plant number one is getting enough water to survive? Why not? Why is plant number two healthy? Where does water enter a plant?

WHAT'S HAPPENING HERE? Plant roots have many tiny hairlike projections called ROOT HAIRS. Root hairs absorb the water and minerals plants need from the soil.

WHICH WAY?

How does water get from the roots to the leaves?

Materials:

glass jar
2 stalks of celery with leaves

red food coloring

pen knife
ruler

1. Fill the jar with water and add a few drops of food coloring. Cut about an inch from the bottom of the celery and put the stalk in the water.

2. Check the stalk every half hour. What is happening? Can you see the food coloring traveling inside the stem? If you leave the celery in the jar for a while longer, will the coloring reach the leaves? Try it.

3. Remove the stalk and cut another inch from the bottom. The small circles you see are the ends of fluid-filled tubes that run the length of the plant. These tubes are what carry the water to the leaves. The water in the tubes also keeps the plant stem firm.

4. Pour out the colored water and wash the jar. Place the second stalk of celery in direct sunlight for a few hours. What happened to the water in the celery? Without water to support the stem how is the celery different?

5. Fill the jar with fresh cool water and place the stalk in it. Leave it for an hour or so. Is the celery any different? Why?

> **WHAT'S HAPPENING HERE?** Tiny tubes, called XYLEM (zī-lem), in the stems and leaves of a green plant transport the water from the roots. Water is drawn up from the roots and carried to every part of the plant where it is needed. The water inside the xylem also helps to support the plant and keep it firm.

WAY OUT

How does the water leave a plant?

Materials:

small plastic bag   potted geranium   twist tie

Procedure:

1. Put the plastic bag over several leaves and tie it off near the stem as close to the soil as possible.

2. Leave the plant in a sunny window for two or three hours. What happens?
3. Open the bag. What is inside? Where did the water come from? Do you think that the leaves that are not covered are also releasing water into the air?

WHAT'S HAPPENING HERE? Not all of the water taken in by a plant is used in the process of photosynthesis. In most green, leafy plants excess water seeps out through the stomata. The Stomata are tiny openings—not visible by the naked eye—which are located in the Epidermise of the plant leaves. This process is called TRANSPIRATION.

TURN ON THE LIGHTS

Do plants need light?

Materials:

4 potted plants   petroleum jelly   stapler
white paper

Procedure:

1. Mark one plant number one and put it in a closet out of the light. Mark another plant number two and put it in a sunny window. For three or four days, care for each plant in the same way. What happens? Does the soil in one stay wetter? Which one? Does one plant look better than the other? Why?

2. Move the sick plant into the light. Do you think it will recover?

3. On plant number two, coat the top of one leaf with petroleum jelly so nothing but light can enter. Staple a piece of paper around another leaf on the same plant. Which leaf will do better? Why?

4. Mark the last two plants three and four. Keep both in a closet. Expose one to light for a few hours only in the morning. Give the other plant light only in the afternoon. Is there a difference?

WHAT'S HAPPENING HERE? The energy green plants use to produce food comes from light. Without light photosynthesis cannot take place and the plants will die.

TOWARD THE LIGHT

Do plant leaves always grow upward?

Materials:

6 fresh lima beans   large glass jar   blotting paper
paper towels

Procedure:

Procedure: **13**

1. Begin by soaking the beans overnight in water.

2. The following day, line the inside of the jar with blotting paper. Stuff paper towels into the center and fill it with water. Wait five minutes then drain off the water.

3. Put the beans between the blotting paper and the jar. Place each one at a different angle. Keep the jar in a closet for two to three days. Be sure to keep the blotting paper and paper towels moist so that the beans will sprout. Since the beans are all in different angles, will the stems grow in different directions? The roots?

4. Observe the jar after two or three days. Did you guess correctly? Turn the jar on its side and wait a day or two before you check it again. What happens to the roots and stems now?

WHAT'S HAPPENING HERE? There are hormones in the tips of plant roots that are sensitive to Earth's gravitational pull and cause the roots to grow downward. Hormones in the tip of the stem are sensitive to light. That is why plants will grow toward a sunny window. This reaction is called TROPISM.

MEAL TIME

Do all plants use photosynthesis to make food?

Materials:

2 large glass   2 1-foot-long   clay
   jars with lids   pieces of   measuring
measuring cup   rubber tubing   spoon
sugar   flour   marking pen
          2 glasses   2 clothespins

1 package of baker's yeast (a simple plant)

Procedure:

1. Punch a hole in one of the jar lids large enough to slip in the tubing. Seal the hole with a ball of clay.

2. Mix one cup of flour with one tablespoon of sugar, one-quarter package of yeast, and one-half cup of water. Knead this into a dough and put it in the bottom of the jar with the hole in the lid. Mark this jar number one. Screw on the lid tightly.

3. Mix another batch of dough for the second jar marked number two, but this time leave out the sugar. Place both jars in a warm spot.

4. Check the jars after two hours. What has happened? Did the dough behave differently in one jar from the

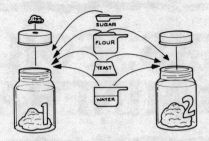

other? What was different about the preparation? What was the food consumed by the active yeast?

5. What caused the bread to rise? Fill a glass with limewater. Remove the lid from jar number one. Remove the clay, slip in the tube, and pack clay around the edges. Clip the end of the tube shut with a clothespin.

6. Puncture several holes in the dough and rapidly replace the lid. Remove the clothespin from the tube and, as quickly as you can, place the open end of the tube in the glass of limewater. If the limewater turns milky, then the gas carbon dioxide is present. What happens?

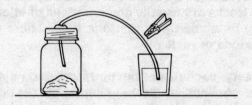

WHAT'S HAPPENING HERE? CHLOROPHYLL is the green pigment in plants where sugars are produced. Some plants, such as fungi, do not have chlorophyll and cannot produce their own food. The yeast in this experiment used the sugar in the first batch of bread dough for food and gave off carbon dioxide as a by-product.

ROCKS, SOIL AND MINERALS

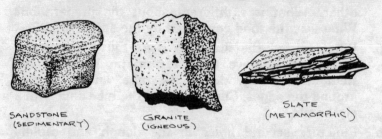

SANDSTONE
(SEDIMENTARY)

GRANITE
(IGNEOUS)

SLATE
(METAMORPHIC)

When Earth formed about 4.5 billion years ago, it was a swirling ball of molten rock. Eventually it cooled and hardened, forming a thin crust called the LITHOSPHERE. The crust is made up of rocks and minerals. Minerals are non-living substances that occur naturally in the Earth, have a certain chemical composition, and usually form in crystals. Calcite and quartz are minerals, as are copper and gold. Rocks are usually combinations of minerals, but some may be made up of just one type. There are three different kinds of rock.

Sedimentary rocks are the most common type. They form over millions of years, when tiny particles from minerals, plants, and animals are pressed and cemented together. Limestone, sandstone, and coal are sedimentary rocks.

Igneous rocks form when molten magma (rock material) from deep within Earth cools and hardens. Granite and basalt are examples of igneous rocks.

Metamorphic rocks are those that are changed from one type of rock to another usually by great heat and pressure. Marble is an example of metamorphic rock, which is formed from limestone.

HARDNESS

How hard is rock?

Materials:

penny
steel file
blackboard
  chalk

tailor's chalk
  (or talc)
nail
notebook

pencil lead
  (graphite)
emery paper

Procedure:

1. Some rocks, minerals, and their products are harder than others. To test this you must make a scale of hardness. Scientists use a scale called Mohs' scale, which grades various minerals from one to ten. You can make your own scale.

2. Begin with the penny. Use it to try to scratch the other objects. Put the things that can be scratched by the penny on one side and those that cannot on the other side.

3. From one pile select an object and test it against the others in the pile. Some will be harder. Some will be softer. Continue to do this until each object has a place in line, harder than the neighbor on one side and softer than the neighbor on the other.

4. Assign the first object, probably the tailor's chalk, number one. Each other object gets a number according to its place in line. Record your results in the notebook. Now you have made a scale to test other objects against. What will you name your scale?

WHAT'S HAPPENING HERE? The hardness of a substance depends on how close the atoms in the substance are to each other and how strongly they are attracted to each other. If the attraction is weak, the material is more easily scratched.

CRYSTALS

How do crystals form?

Materials:

tall glass jar	spoon	sugar
food coloring	1 foot of light	paper clip
pencil	string	

Procedure:

1. Fill the jar with very hot water. Stir in sugar, a spoonful at a time, until no more will dissolve in the water. Add a few drops of food coloring.

2. Tie one end of the string around the middle of the pencil and attach the paper clip to the other end. Lower the string into the jar. Turn the pencil to shorten the string until the paper clip hangs an inch from the bottom.

3. Let the jar set for a few days. Crystals will form. The longer you wait, the larger the crystals will grow. Are the crystals made of sugar? Taste them. This is how rock candy is made. Crystals can be made from salt, too.

WHAT'S HAPPENING HERE? When certain substances form, the atoms become arranged in an orderly pattern. This pattern is the CRYSTAL STRUCTURE. As more atoms are attracted and join this structure, the crystal "grows." Crystals form in one of two ways, evaporation or cooling. By stirring the sugar into hot water you break down the crystals. As the water cools, the crystals reform.

BENEATH YOUR FEET

What is soil made of?

Materials:

6 glass jars with lids
marking pen

small spade
6 stick-on labels
magnifying glass

soil
kitchen bulb
siphon

Procedure:

1. Fill each jar with three inches of soil, each sample collected from a different place. Put a label on the jar and write the place where the sample was collected. Note the type of plants that were growing in the soil and any other interesting characteristics. Were there any animals living in the soil?

2. When all of the samples have been collected, fill each jar with water and shake well. What happens to the water? Allow each sample to settle. Check them every hour. The contents of which jar settled first? Did the soil form layers? The heaviest elements in the soil will have settled first and be on the bottom.

3. Siphon out as much water as possible, then set the jars in a sunny spot. The rest of the water will evaporate.

4. When the soil has dried, take a sample from each layer to examine under the magnifying glass. How is each layer different? Do they feel different? Is soil made up of a combination of things?

WHAT'S HAPPENING HERE? Soil is formed from weathered rock and minerals. The type of soil depends on a number of things, including the original rock, the climate, and the plants that were in the area as the soil formed.

SOGGY SOIL

Which holds more water, sandy soil or clay soil?

Materials:

2 paper cups   sandy soil   clay soil
2 measuring cups

1. Make a small hole in the bottom of each cup. Fill one cup with sandy soil and the other with clay soil.

2. Fill one measuring cup to half full with water. Hold the paper cup filled with clay soil over the empty measuring cup and pour the water over the soil. Wait until it stops draining. Note how much water poured through.

3. Repeat the procedure, this time with sandy soil. Which one held the most water? Do you think that different kinds of plants need different kinds of soil? Do plants that need little water grow best in sandy or clay soil? Why?

EROSION

DISAPPEARING SOIL*

Does rain erode soil?

Materials:

hammer	nail	coffee can
newspaper	1 cup of small	cookie tin with
soil to fill the	pebbles	raised edges
cookie tin	pitcher of water	clay
5 small wide-leafed artificial plants		

Procedure:

1. Have a parent help you. With the hammer and the nail, punch many small holes in the bottom of the coffee can. Spread the newspaper on a flat surface out of doors. Put a layer of pebbles in the bottom of the cookie tin and top it with a layer of soil. Place the cookie tin on the newspaper so that it is slightly tilted.

2. Hold the coffee can over the cookie tin. Pour the water into the can. Let it rain down on the slope you have created. What happens to the soil? What is left if you continue to pour rain on the slope? Can rainwater cause soil erosion?

3. Set up your slope again but this time, before you add the soil, place several balls of clay on the tray to hold

4. Is there less soil erosion when plants are on the slope?
    Would a layer of grass hold the soil in place? During a
    heavy rainfall, what would happen to a hillside on
    which a fire has destroyed the plants and grass?

CRACKED ROCKS*

Can temperature changes cause erosion?

Materials:

clear plastic jar
small rock
rubber gloves
newspapers

tongs
magnifying
 glass
bowl

pot holder
balloon
plaster of paris
notebook

Procedure:

1. Erosion is the wearing away of rocks and soil. Fill the jar with cool water. With the tongs, hold a small rock over an open flame until it is very hot. Put the rock into the cool water. What happens? Examine the rock with the magnifying glass. Do cracks form?

2. Fill the balloon with water and tie it closed.

3. Wearing rubber gloves, make a thick plaster of paris mixture in the bowl according to directions. Form a ball around the balloon several layers thick. Put the balloon on the newspaper so that you don't make a big mess.

4. Place the covered balloon in the freezer overnight. What happened when the water in the balloon froze? What would happen if rainwater filled a crack in a rock and froze?

WHAT'S HAPPENING HERE? Generally, heat caus- es things to expand and cold causes things to con- tract. The rapid heating and cooling of a material weakens it and it may crack. This may happen to rocks in a desert that bake by day and become very cold at night. Water is the only material that expands when it freezes. If water freezes in a crack, it can put tremendous pressure on this already weak point in the rock.

Wind can also cause erosion. So can pollution. Walk around your neighborhood and look for examples of erosion. Keep a list in your notebook of the type of erosion you find and what might have caused it.

CARVING CAVES

How are caves formed?

Materials:

measuring cup   bottle of plain   2 pieces of
marking pen   soda water   granite
saucepan   2 glass jars   spoon
2 pieces of limestone (available at rock shops or
  garden supply stores)

Procedure:

1. Boil 2 cups of water in a saucepan to purify it. Let the water cool then pour it into one of the jars. Mark the jar number one.

2. Fill a jar marked number two with soda water. Stir the soda water until the bubbles are gone. Let it set for a while then stir again.

3. Put a piece of limestone and a piece of granite in each jar. What happens? How are the reactions different? The soda water in jar two is slightly acidic. It reacts with the calcite and will finally dissolve it. Do you think there is calcite in the granite?

4. How can rainwater effect areas made up of granite and limestone?

WHAT'S HAPPENING HERE? CALCITE is a form of calcium carbonate. Limestone is made up mostly of calcite. Rainwater becomes slightly acidic as it seeps through the soil. It can slowly dissolve underground calcite deposits, leaving caverns.

WATER SCULPTURE*

How do stalactites form in caves?

Materials:

2 glass jars
small plate
Epsom salts

8 inches of
heavy wool
knitting yarn

spoon
potholders

Procedure:

1. Have a parent help you fill both jars with very hot water. Stir in Epsom salts one spoonful at a time, until the water <u>can</u> hold no more.

2. Place the jars where they will not be disturbed. Put the small plate between them, and put one end of the wool strand in each jar. After three or four days, check your experiment. What is happening? What is your stalagmite made of? Will the columns on the bottom and top eventually meet? Try it.

WHAT'S HAPPENING HERE? The water and dissolved Epsom salts in the jars are absorbed by the wool. As the water collects in the center of the strand, it will begin to drip very slowly. As each drop hangs from the wool, the water begins to evaporate leaving behind the salts, which build up after a while. Some drops may fall to the plate and a salt formation will grow there, too. It is through this same process that cones and columns form in caves. A STALACTITE forms on the roof of a cave. The formation on the floor of a cave is a STALAGMITE.

ROCKS FROM LIVING THINGS

Do all rocks and minerals contain carbonates?

Materials:

file	hammer	limestone
baking soda	real chalk	marble
eggshell	seashell	different kinds
salt	bowl	of rocks
eyedropper		vinegar

1. Certain rocks—chalk, for instance—are made up of the remains, such as shells, of living creatures. (Blackboard chalk is usually made up of another material called gypsum. Real chalk can be obtained from a paint store.) These rocks and some other rocks and minerals contain carbonates.

2. To find out if there are carbonates in a material, file a small portion of the object you are testing or crack it with the hammer. If possible, crush the object or a piece of it and place it in the bowl.

3. Using the eyedropper drop several drops of vinegar on the material you are testing. What happens? Does it fizz or bubble? If so, the object contains carbonates. Test the other materials.

WHAT IS HAPPENING HERE? The bubbling is caused when carbonates come in contact with a weak acid such as vinegar and carbon dioxide is released.

WATER

Living things on Earth need water to survive. More than seventy percent of the surface of our planet is covered by water, which makes up the HYDROSPHERE.

Most of this is salt water in the oceans and seas. Another two percent is frozen into the ice and snow of Earth's polar regions. The rest is fresh water in lakes and rivers, groundwater, and vapor in the air.

HEAVY WATER

Which is heavier, fresh or salt water?

Materials:

2 pop bottles	measuring	3 × 5 card
food coloring	spoons	salt

1. Fill one bottle with water, add three teaspoons of salt, and shake it. Fill the second bottle with water. Add some food coloring to this bottle.

2. Place the 3 × 5 card over the opening of the bottle containing salty water. Hold the card in place with your hand and turn the bottle over.

3. Balance this bottle on top of the one containing fresh water. Carefully slip the card out from between.
What happens? The heaviest solution will drift to the bottom. Is salty water heavier?

> **WHAT'S HAPPENING HERE? DENSITY** is the ratio of weight to volume. If two substances are of the same volume but one is more dense, the denser substance will be heavier. Seawater is more dense because in each volume of water there is the weight of the water plus the additional weight of the dissolved salts.

SALTY RAIN

Why doesn't water from the ocean fall as salty rain?

Materials:

large tub at
  least 6 inches
  high
spoon

measuring cup
glass pint jar
small rock
tape

salt
large plastic
  trash bag

Procedure:

1. Fill the tub with three inches of water, pour in one-half cup of salt, enough to make the water taste salty. Put the tub where it will be in direct sunlight for most of the day.

2. Set the jar in the center of the tub. Cover the top of the tub completely with the plastic trash bag. Tape the bag in place. Put the rock in the center so that it weights the plastic down toward the glass. The bag must not touch the glass. What will happen as the water heats up?

3. As the water evaporates, it cannot escape but instead will condense on the plastic and flow toward the glass. Does salt evaporate in sunlight? Will there be salt water in the glass or fresh water?

4. At the end of the day, take out the glass and taste the water. Did you answer correctly? Where is the salt? Why?

WHAT IS HAPPENING HERE? As it warms, the water in the tub evaporates, leaving the salt behind.

DEEP WATER

Is deep ocean water usually warmer or colder than water at the surface?

Materials:

tray of ice
gallon glass jar
   with a wide
   mouth

2 feet of string
food coloring
rubber band

eyedropper
small glass
   bottle

Procedure:

1. Fill the ice tray with water tinted with several drops of food coloring. Freeze it overnight.

2. Fill the gallon jar with very cold water. Loop the rubber band around the lip of the small bottle. Tie each end of the string to the rubber band so that the bottle can be lifted without tipping.

3. Fill the small bottle with hot water and add a few drops of food coloring. Lower the bottle carefully by the string into the cold water jar. What happens? Can

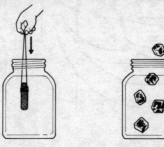

you see swirls of colored water rising from the bottle? Does the warm colored water mix with the rest of the water? Where does the warm water go?

FREEZING POINT

Does ocean and fresh water freeze at the same temperature?

Materials:

2 plastic
  margarine
  containers

marking pen
thermometer
salt

measuring
spoons

Procedure:

1. Mark one container number one and fill it with water.
2. Mark the second container number two. Fill it with water. Stir 2 teaspoons of salt into the water. Record the temperature of the water in each container, then put both in the freezer.

3. Check the temperature of each container of water **35**
    every hour. Which container freezes first? Which has
    a lower freezing point?

WHAT'S HAPPENING HERE? Pure water freezes at
32° Fahrenheit. Water with dissolved salts does not
freeze until 28.6° Fahrenheit. Sodium and chlorine
are the two most plentiful elements in seawater. They
combine to make sodium chloride or common salt.

FLOATING ICE

Why do icebergs float?

Materials:

1 plastic margarine container with lid
measuring   2 glass bowls
  spoons   salt
tray of ice

Procedure:

1. Fill the margarine container
    to the rim with water.
    Put the lid on the
    container and freeze it
    overnight. Does the ice take
    up more or less room
    than the same amount
    of water? Do you think
    ice is lighter or heavier
    than the same amount of water?

2. Fill one bowl with fresh water. Fill the second bowl with water, add two teaspoons of salt, and stir.

3. Place an ice cube in each bowl. Look very carefully. Does the ice cube in the salt water float slightly higher than the cube in fresh water? Why? Why do icebergs float in the ocean? Can the lower freezing point of salt water help an iceberg to last longer?

WHAT IS HAPPENING HERE? When water freezes, the molecules line up in such a way that there is more space between them than when they are in liquid form. The ice expands and takes up more space. For this reason, the same volume of ice weighs less than the same volume of water.

WEATHER

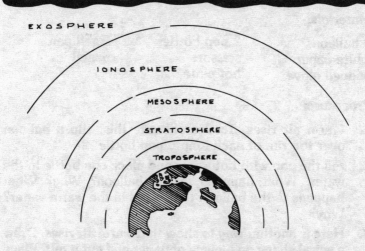

EXOSPHERE

IONOSPHERE

MESOSPHERE

STRATOSPHERE

TROPOSPHERE

Protective gases, mostly nitrogen and oxygen, surround Earth and make up the ATMOSPHERE. The atmosphere includes four main layers and a thin outer layer.

The **exosphere** is the very thin outermost layer.

The **ionosphere** is between thirty and three hundred miles above Earth. Temperatures here can vary from -1120° Fahrenheit at lower levels to more than 2500° Fahrenheit.

Mesosphere: a layer of the atmosphere extending from the top of the stratosphere to an altitude of about 50 miles.

The **stratosphere** lies between thirty miles to about ten miles above Earth's surface. Within this area of the atmosphere is the protective *ozone layer* that absorbs dangerous radiation from the Sun.

The **troposphere** is the layer nearest Earth. It holds most of the planet's water vapor. Within the troposphere are strong, high-level winds called *jet streams* that have much influence on Earth's climates and on changeable weather.

MOVING AIR

What is wind?

Materials:

2 balloons
white paper
padded glove

2 pop bottles
scissors
hot plate

small pan
pencil

Procedure:

1. Warm air rises. To demonstrate this, slip a balloon over the rim of each empty pop bottle.

2. Fill the pan with hot water and place one bottle in the water. What happens to the balloon? Why? What happens to the balloon that is not in the warm water? Why?

3. Here is another way to show that warm air rises. Draw a spiral shape on a piece of paper and cut it out. Place the end of the spiral over the pencil tip. Wearing the padded glove, turn the hot plate on high and hold the pencil above the hot plate. What happens to the paper spiral? Why?

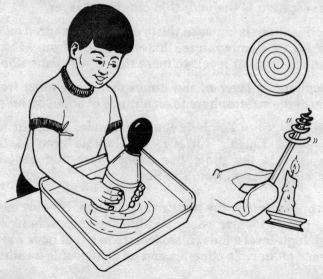

WHAT'S HAPPENING HERE? Warm air rises. By putting the pop bottle in the hot water you are heating the air inside. Wind is the movement of air. One cause of this movement is the uneven heating of the atmosphere by the Sun. As the warm air rises, cooler air moves in to take its place. This may be felt as wind.

CHILLY MEETING

Does cold air sink?

Materials:

6 to 8 ice cubes   plastic bag   measuring
salt   twist tie   spoons
thermometer   2 pencils   oatmeal box

Procedure:

1. Lightly crush the ice and put it in the plastic bag. Add one teaspoon of salt and seal the bag.

2. Make a small hole in the bottom of the oatmeal box and insert the thermometer. Note the temperature of the air in the box.

3. Put the pencils across the open top of the box and rest the bag of ice on them. Wait fifteen minutes and read the temperature again. Is it cooler? Why? Does the warm air begin to cool as it passes the ice?

WHAT'S HAPPENING HERE? Cool air, being more dense, is heavier than warm air. Even though the ice is not in the box, the cooler air around it will sink and the temperature in the box will lower.

STICKY WEATHER

Why are hot, humid days more uncomfortable than hot, dry days?

Materials:

glass	paper towel	thermometer
twist tie		blotting paper

Procedure:

1. Fill the glass with water that is the same temperature as the room. Tear a small strip from the paper towel, dip it in the water, and wrap it around the bulb of the thermometer. Hold the strip in place with the twist tie. Record the temperature. Has it changed?

2.   Put the thermometer in the glass of water and record the temperature after five minutes.

3.   Line the glass with a piece of blotting paper. Wait a moment, then pour out the water. In the air of the room, wrapping the thermometer in a moist towel made the temperature drop. Will the same thing happen in the moisture-filled air in the glass? Try it.

WHAT'S HAPPENING HERE? Water vapor in the air is called HUMIDITY. The evaporation of water from your skin as sweat has a cooling effect, but the air can only hold a certain amount of water. When humidity is high, sweat will stay on your skin and you will feel sticky and uncomfortable.

FOG IN A BOTTLE

How does fog form?

Materials:

clear glass pop   1 ice cube   plastic wrap
  or juice bottle

Procedure:

1. Fill the bottle with hot water. Let it set for a moment. Pour out most of the water leaving about an inch in the bottle.

2. Put the ice cube on the top of the bottle. What happens as the warm, moist air meets the cold air?

3. Cover the ice in plastic wrap and repeat the experiment. Did the fog appear? Is the water vapor from which the fog forms in the ice or in the warm air?

WHAT'S HAPPENING HERE? The warm air in the bottle holds water vapor. It is cooled when it comes in contact with the ice. The water vapor condenses onto particles in the air, forming tiny droplets that you see as fog.

DEW POINT

At what temperature will water vapor condense?

Materials:

shiny metal   paper towel   thermometer
  coffee can
6 to 8 ice cubes

1. Fill the can ¾ full with water. Carefully dry the outside of the can.

2. Stirring with the thermometer, add the ice one cube at a time. Allow each ice cube to melt before adding the next. Note the temperature when drops begin to form on the outside of the can. Where does the water on the outside come from? The temperature at which water vapor condenses is called the dew point.

3. Do you think the dew point is always the same? Repeat this experiment on several different days. Compare the temperatures. Try the experiment on a cloudy day or at night. Does this make a difference?

WHAT IS HAPPENING HERE? As air becomes cool, it is unable to hold as much water vapor as warm air. The air around the can is slowly cooled to the point that the water condenses and droplets form on the chilled surface of the can.

APRIL SHOWERS

How does rain form?

Materials:

metal pot	metal pie pan	12 ice cubes
padded glove	marking pen	

Procedure:

1. Fill the pot with water and bring it to a steady boil. Can you see the water vapor rising into the air?

2. Fill the pie pan with ice and some water. Wearing the padded glove to protect your hand, hold the pie pan about six inches above the pot. What happens to the water vapor when it touches the bottom of the pan? Why?

3. The droplets on the pie pan will fall when they become heavy enough. What happens to water vapor carried upwards in currents of warm air? Where does water vapor in the air come from?

4. Remove the ice cubes from the pie pan. Mark the level of the water in the pan and place it in a sunny window for a few days. What happens? Is the water level lower? Where has it gone?

45

WHAT IS HAPPENING HERE? When warm air encounters the very cold air of the upper atmosphere, water vapor condenses onto smoke or dust particles and freezes into small ice crystals. As the ice crystals collect, clouds develop. When the crystals become too heavy they begin to fall back to Earth. If the temperature is low enough, they will fall as snow or hail. Usually they melt in the warmer lower atmosphere and fall as rain.

WHAT GOES UP MUST COME DOWN*

What is the rain cycle?

Materials:

| 3 small potted plants | 2 metal cookie trays | hot plate |
| teakettle | padded glove | 12 ice cubes |

Procedure:

1. Place the plants in one tray next to the hot plate. Fill the teakettle with water, place it on the hot plate, and bring it to a boil with the spout facing toward the tray.
2. Fill the second tray with ice and some water. Hold it

above the plants and close enough to the teakettle so that water vapor will reach it.

3. The teakettle represents the source of the water vapor, such as an ocean or lake. The upper tray is cold air in the atmosphere. What will happen as the water vapor condenses? What will finally happen to the water that has fallen on the small plants as rain?

WHAT IS HAPPENING HERE? Water is constantly evaporating from the surface of Earth's great bodies of water. The water vapor is carried by warm air high into the upper atmosphere. At this point the air cools, the water vapor condenses and, when conditions are right, falls as rain. Some of the rainwater may be absorbed by plants and released back into the air through transpiration. (Transpiration is the passage of water vapor from a living body.) Most of it finds its way to streams, rivers, lakes, and oceans, and the cycle begins again.

YOUR WEATHER STATION

The most important thing to do is to keep good records. Take daily readings of temperature. Note cloud and wind

THE WIND VANE*
(used to tell wind direction)

Materials:

1 piece of wood,   small handsaw   thin board
   6 inches long   glass   tongs
   by ½ inch   eyedropper   drill
   wide   hammer   marking pen
glue   compass
2-inch headless nail
1 piece of wood, 1 inch square and 1 foot long

Procedure:

1. Make a small slit about one inch deep in each end of the six-inch piece of wood. From the thin board cut shapes that look like those in the illustration, then slip them into the slots and glue them securely.

2. Seal the small end of the eyedropper by turning it over a low flame. Hold the glass with tongs so you don't burn your fingers.

3. Drive the nail into the top of the foot-long piece of wood. Find the spot on your arrow at which it will balance on the nail without falling. Mark that spot and drill a small hole there a little wider than the end of the eyedropper.

4. Slip the eyedropper over the nail and insert the other end into the hole in the arrow. It should spin freely. Mount your wind vane in an open area.

Aim your compass in the direction the arrow is pointing to determine the direction of the wind.

THE BAROMETER
(used to gauge air pressure)

Materials:

1 balloon	scissors	large jar
rubber band	glue	1 plastic straw
3 × 5 card	marking pen	

Procedure:

1. Cut a section from the balloon. Stretch it over the top of the jar using the rubber band to hold it in place. Put a drop of glue in the center of the balloon. Attach the straw horizontally by one end.

2. Put the jar on a tabletop near a wall. Pin the white card to the wall next to the jar. Write the word *high* above

the level of the straw. When the air pressure is high it will push down on the balloon causing the straw "indicator" to point to high.

THE NEPHOSCOPE
(used to determine how fast and what direction the wind is blowing high above the earth)

Materials:

measuring tape   compass   glue
mirror 6 inches   paintbrush   white paint
  in diameter
piece of cardboard 8 inches in diameter

Procedure:

1. Glue the mirror in the center of the cardboard so there is an even border all the way around it. Use the measuring tape to find the center of the mirror and put a dot of white paint there. On the border, write an N for north, an S for south and so on, as shown in the sample.

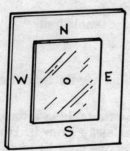

2. Put your nethoscope on a flat surface outside. Use the compass to be sure that the N is facing directly north. As a cloud passes across the mirror, note which direction it has come from.

3. Use a stopwatch, or a watch with a second hand, to time how long it takes for the edge of the cloud to travel across the mirror.

THE SUN AND THE MOON

EARTH'S NEIGHBORS

Why does the Moon have phases?

Materials:

knitting needle   tennis ball   lamp

Procedure:

1. Push the knitting needle into the ball to use as a handle.
2. Place the lamp on a table in a darkened room. Stand about three feet away from it. Hold the ball by the needle slightly above your head so that the light falls on it. You represent Earth. The lamp is the Sun and the tennis ball is the Moon. Stand with your back to the light. The tennis ball is completely lit. Now slowly turn in a circle watching the ball. How does it change? What happens when you are facing the lamp?
3. What would happen if you (Earth) were to pass between the Sun and the Moon? Try it. The darkening of the Moon in this manner is called a lunar eclipse.

What do you think would happen if the Moon moved between your view from Earth of the Sun? Solar eclipses are not visible to everyone on Earth at the same time. Why?

WHAT'S HAPPENING HERE? Half of the Moon is always lit by the sun. The Moon takes about thirty days to orbit around Earth. We see different amounts of the sunlit portion of the Moon depending on its position in orbit around us.

PERMANENT ICE

Why don't the polar ice caps melt away?

Materials:

black paint	white paint	paintbrush
2 coffee cans	thermometer	

Procedure:

1. Paint the outside of one can black, the other white. Fill both cans with water.

2. Place both cans in the Sun and record the temperature of the water. An hour later which can do you think will contain hotter water?

3. Test it. Which one was hotter? Bright surfaces reflect heat while dark surfaces absorb it. Would a field of bright snow absorb or reflect the warm rays of the Sun?

WHAT'S HAPPENING HERE? The rate at which a surface reflects light is called its ALBEDO. Dark surfaces have a low albedo while bright snow has a very high albedo. Instead of being absorbed, much of the heat radiation that can cause the temperature to rise is reflected away. The larger the ice field, the greater this effect becomes. Of course, some of the ice and snow melts and the ice caps become smaller in summer, but they never melt away completely.

RED SKY AT NIGHT

Why is the sky at sunset sometimes red?

Materials:

glass jar   flashlight   milk

Procedure:

1. Fill the glass jar with water. In a darkened room, hold the flashlight level with the center of the glass jar and shine the light into the water. What color does the water appear? The water is scattering the light and reflecting blue light to your eye. The same thing happens when light is scattered by the atmosphere. That is why the sky looks blue during the day.

2. Now move so that you are on the opposite side of the glass jar from the flashlight. Does the color change when you are looking at the light through the water?

3. Pour some milk into the glass jar. Look at the water from the same side as the flashlight. Does it appear blue again?

4. Move so that you are once again looking at the light through the water. Now what color do you see?

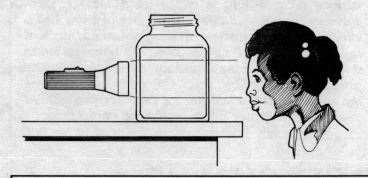

WHAT IS HAPPENING HERE? The milk represents dust and water vapor in the atmosphere. When the Sun is low on the horizon, its light falls at a different angle and often only the red light reaches your eye.

THE FOUR SEASONS

Why are there seasons on Earth?

Materials:

marking pen   tennis ball   knitting needle
lamp

Procedure:

1. Draw a line around the middle of the ball to represent the equator. Put a large dot on the equator. Put another dot an inch above the first and one an inch below the first. These dots represent cities. Push the

knitting needle through the top of the ball and out the
other side. This is Earth's axis.

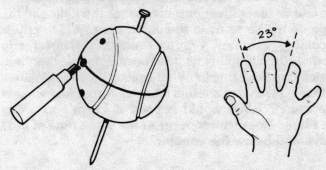

2. Put the lamp in the center of a darkened room. Stand about two feet away from the lamp. With one end of the knitting needle, hold the ball even with the bulb.

3. Earth is slightly tilted on its axis about twenty-three degrees. Hold your hand so that your index finger points straight up. Spread your fingers as wide as you can. The space between your index and ring fingers is about twenty-three degrees. Hold the needle so that it is at the same angle as your ring finger pointing away from the lamp. Be sure your cities are facing the light. This position represents Earth on December 22. Which city is getting the most light? Which city do

you think is the coldest at this time of year?

4. Move one quarter of the way around the light. Rotate the ball so that cities continue to face the light and the angle is the same as in the illustration. Which city is becoming warmer? Continue another quarter trip around the lamp. Now the needle faces the Sun. Which city is warmest? What season do you think it is in that city? Move another quarter turn. Now what is happening? What would happen if Earth's axis was not tilted? Does winter occur at the same time of year above and below the equator?

WHAT IS HAPPENING HERE? If Earth were not tilted on its axis, there would be no difference in the seasons. Because of the tilt, areas tilted toward the Sun have longer periods of daylight and the rays of the Sun are more direct. As Earth moves in its orbit around the Sun, the same areas become tilted away from the Sun. They then have shorter periods of daylight. The Sun's rays reach them at more of a slant and are not as strong.

GLOSSARY OF SCIENCE WORDS YOU SHOULD KNOW

animal. A living thing that is capable of reproduction and is not a plant.

bedrock. A layer of solid rock below the subsoil.

carbon dioxide. A gas made up of carbon and oxygen atoms.

chlorophyll. A substance in plants that enables them to absorb light from the Sun and use this energy to make food.

climate. The average weather conditions in an area over a long period of time.

cold-blooded. Having a body temperature that changes and adapts to the temperature of the environment.

condensation. The formation of a liquid from a gas by cooling.

crust. The rocky, outer layer of Earth's surface.

eclipse. The casting of a shadow across a body in space by the passing of another body in space.

environment. The surroundings in which plants and animals live.

evaporation. The changing of a liquid to a gas through heat or the motion of air.

fossil. The remains of ancient living things.

groundwater. Water beneath Earth's surface.

metamorphosis. The development of certain animals in four stages from egg to adult.

orbit. The path of an object in space around another object.

photosynthesis. The process green plants use to convert water, sunlight, and carbon dioxide to food.

plant. A living thing that is not an animal.

precipitation. The condensation of water vapor from the atmosphere. Rain, snow, and fog are forms of precipitation.

reproduction. The process by which a living thing produces another organism like itself.

spore. The reproductive cell of certain living things.

topsoil. The uppermost fertile layer of soil on Earth's crust.

warm-blooded. Having a body temperature that is unchanged by the temperature of the environment.